Champ's Story:
Dogs Get Cancer Too!

By Sherry North

Illustrated by Kathleen Rietz

"Ready, set, GO!" Cody yelled.

Champ sprang off the platform and raced through the agility course. She jumped over hurdles, bounded through tunnels, climbed a ladder, and zipped down a slide. *Woof!* she called as she crossed the finish line.

"Fifteen seconds," Cody said. "That's your best time ever. You're going to ace the agility show."

Cody rubbed Champ's belly while she rested. His hand slid over a strange bump beneath her soft fur. "What's this, Champ? I never noticed it before."

Champ thumped her tail against the grass.

"Maybe we should see your doctor," Cody said.

When they walked into the vet's office, Champ whined and put her tail between her legs. "I know you don't like coming here," Cody said, "but we'll be done soon."

When the tests were finished, the doctor had some bad news. "Champ has cancer," she explained. "Like people, a dog's body is made of tiny blobs called cells. Sometimes these cells grow the wrong way and make the body sick."

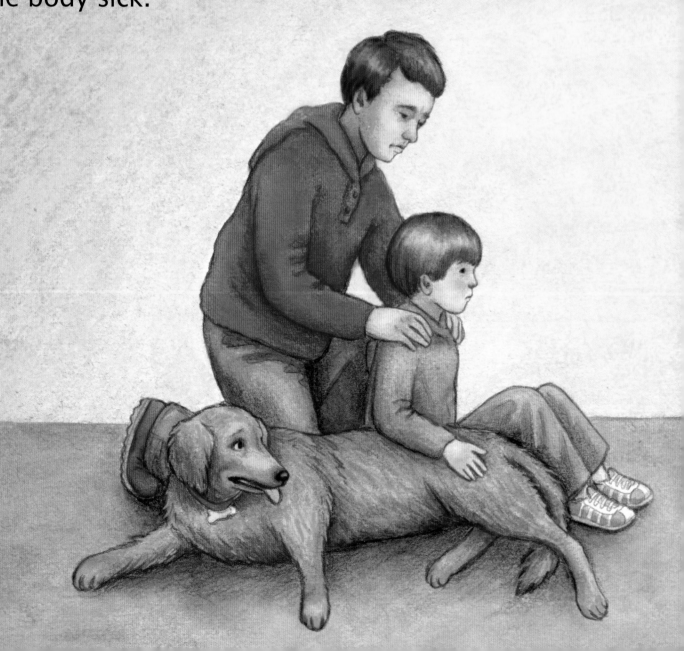

Cody looked into Champ's eyes. "She doesn't seem sick."
"That's the strange thing about cancer," the doctor said.
"Patients can seem fine even though they're sick inside."
Cody's throat felt tight. "Will she be all right?" he asked.
"We have strong medicines to fight the cancer," the vet
answered. "But she will have to come here every week,
and she won't like it."

At home, Cody set out Champ's food and a fresh bowl of water. Then he had a terrible thought. What if this was his fault? Maybe he should never have fed Champ his peanut butter and jelly crusts. Maybe he shouldn't have given her that old sneaker to chew.

Cody lay down on the floor and whispered, "I'm sorry if I did this to you."

Champ licked the tears off Cody's face. She licked his forehead, his cheeks, and his nose.

Cody giggled. "Ugh, Champ, you smell like dog food!"

Champ wagged her tail. She obviously didn't blame Cody. Maybe he didn't make her sick, Cody thought. But he could help her get better.

"When you go in for your medicine, I'm going with you."

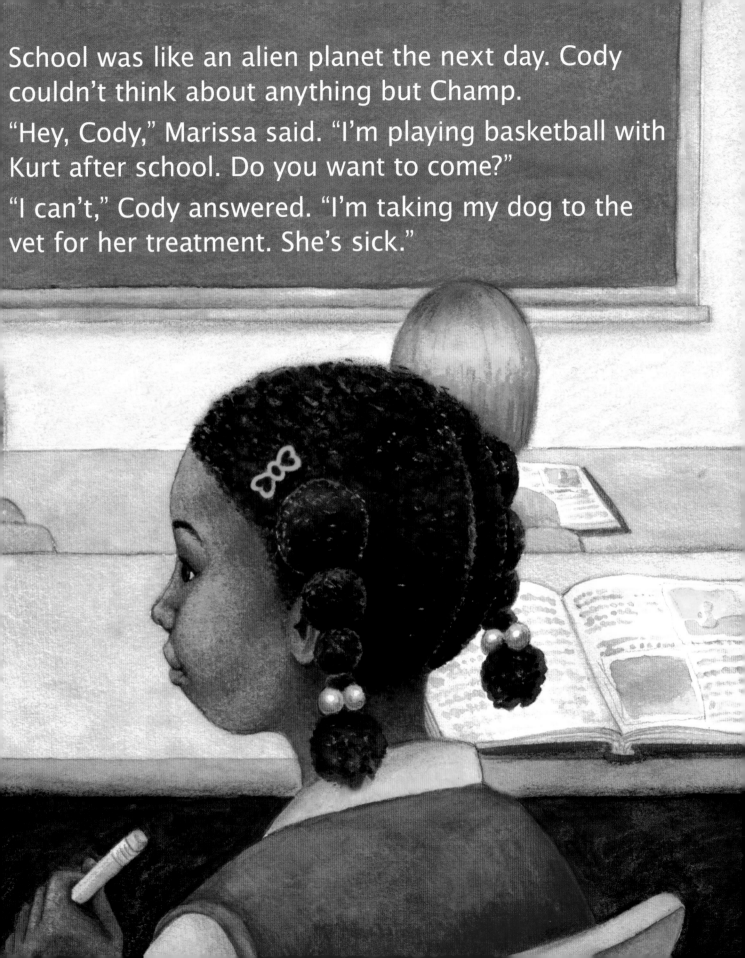

School was like an alien planet the next day. Cody couldn't think about anything but Champ.

"Hey, Cody," Marissa said. "I'm playing basketball with Kurt after school. Do you want to come?"

"I can't," Cody answered. "I'm taking my dog to the vet for her treatment. She's sick."

Cody walked Champ into the chemotherapy room. A nurse set up a clear tube called an IV. The tube pumped medicine into Champ's body through an IV port.

"I know this isn't any fun," Cody said. "Just remember we're trying to help you."

He read Champ a scratch-n-sniff book to take her mind off the IV. "*Mmm*, smell this one! It's peanut butter—your favorite."

Champ sniffed the book and sneezed.

Champp had to take pills every day—and they tasted awful!
Luckily, Cody had an idea. "Here, Champ, how would
you like a spoonful of yummy peanut butter?"

One day, Kurt and Marissa came to see Cody after school. "I heard your dog is sick," Kurt said.

"She has cancer," Cody answered. "She's kind of sad today. She doesn't feel like eating."

"You should cheer her up," Marissa suggested. "What does she like to do?"

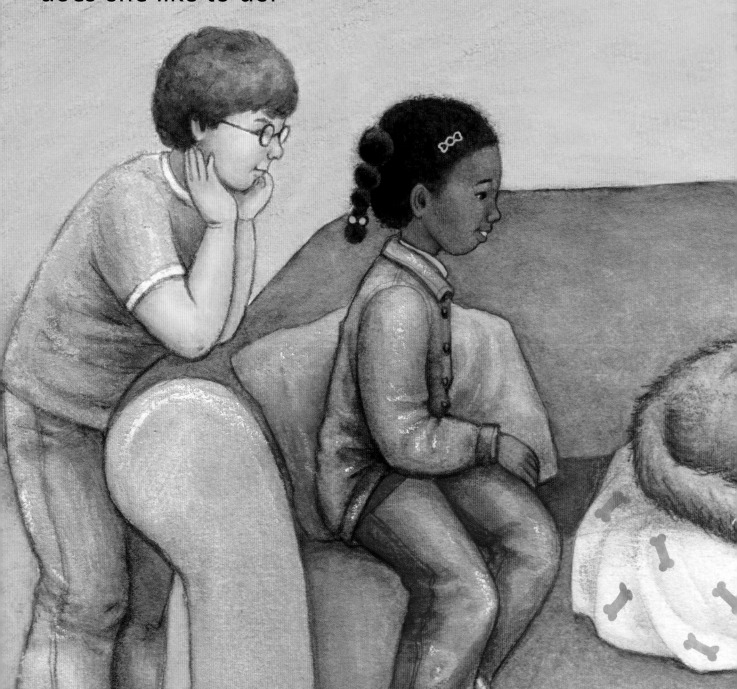

Cody rubbed Champ's belly. "She loves the agility course at Happy Tails Park. But her medicine is making her tired. I don't know if she can run."

"My dog has a bad hip," Kurt said. "I still take her for walks, though. I just go more slowly."

Cody's eyes lit up. "Champ, should we try going to the park?"

Woof! Champ got down off the couch.

Kurt and Marissa cheered as Champ came down the starting platform. Champ was not her graceful self. She ran around the hurdles instead of jumping over them. She skidded down the slide at an odd angle. But she finished the course.

"You did it!" Cody cheered. "Do you want to do another run?"

Champ lay down and put her head on her paws.

"OK, you rest today. We can come back tomorrow."

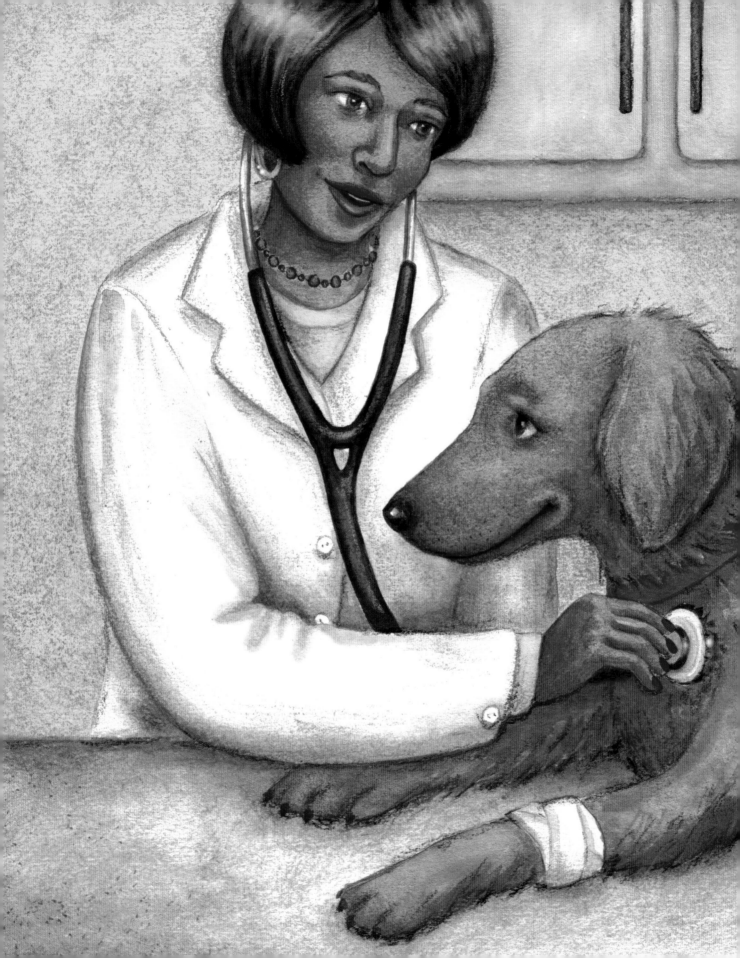

After a few weeks, Champ got a break from her chemotherapy. The doctor did some more tests. "The medicine is helping," she said, "but Champ will have good weeks and bad weeks."

The next week was a good one. Each day, Champ ran a little faster. She jumped onto the starting platform by herself. She raced through the tunnels and leaped a hurdle.

"Yes!" Cody shouted. "With a little practice, we'll be ready for the agility show."

On Saturday, it was show time. Cody jogged alongside Champ as she dashed through the course. He had to run fast to keep up, and he tripped.

"*OWWWWWWW!*" Cody fell to the ground and clutched his ankle. The people watching gasped.

Champ leaped off the ladder and ran straight for Cody. She stood over him, licking his face.

"I can't get up," he stammered.

Champ leaned her body against Cody's side. Cody stood slowly on one foot and hopped, using Champ as a crutch. The crowd cheered as Champ led Cody off the course.

That night, Cody stared at his cast. "I'm sorry, Champ," he said. "I ruined your chance to be a real champion."

Champ jumped onto the bed and snuggled against Cody.

"I guess it's your turn to take care of me, just like I took care of you."

Woof! Champ agreed.

"Maybe you didn't win the title of fastest dog, but you are the bravest."

For Creative Minds

Understanding Cancer

Cancer Cells

Whether you are a person or a puppy, your body is made up of trillions of tiny cells, the body's building blocks. Sometimes, a few cells take on the wrong shape or size and grow out of control. These abnormal cells are known as cancer.

Who Gets Cancer?

Cancer is common in older people (and dogs), but it is not common in children. It's normal for kids with cancer to wonder, "Why me?" No one knows why some kids get cancer, but one thing is certain—it is not because the child did anything wrong.

Chemotherapy (Chemo)

Chemotherapy is a medicine that targets and kills those misbehaving cancer cells. It is usually given through a clear tube called an IV. Chemo sometimes hurts healthy cells, too. This can make patients feel sick to their stomach or lose their hair.

Radiation Therapy

Radiation therapy uses high-energy rays (like strong X-rays) to target and kill the cancer cells. Like chemo, it can sometimes make patients feel worse before they get better. Radiation therapy may be used to treat cancer by itself or along with other treatments, like chemo.

Cancer Research

Medical researchers are doctors who find and test new medications. Thanks to their efforts, cancer treatments are becoming tougher on cancer and easier on the patient. Many groups hold walk-a-thons and other events to raise money for this research.

Cancer True or False

Do you think the following statements are true or false? Answers are upside down on the bottom of the page.

1	You cannot catch cancer from another child, no matter how much you play together.

2	People who need chemotherapy will lose their hair forever.

3	Animals that live in the ocean do not get cancer.

4	Most children with cancer will get better.

5	When dogs get chemotherapy, they lose their fur.

1. TRUE. Cancer is not like a cold or flu. It does not spread from one person to another.

2. FALSE. Chemotherapy can damage the cells that make hair grow. These cells get better when treatment is over, and hair starts to grow again. Children who lose their hair may choose to wear a hat, wig or bandana until it grows back.

3. FALSE. Sea lions, beluga whales, and green sea turtles get cancer. Sharks get cancer too, but not very often.

4. TRUE. Treatments for cancer may not be any fun, but they work. Most children get better and go on to have normal lives.

5. FALSE. A dog's fur grows differently than a person's hair. Most breeds do not lose their fur during chemotherapy (with the exception of poodles and some kinds of terriers). Unfortunately, most people do lose hair during chemo treatments.

Coping with Cancer & Chemo

Children with cancer not only have to deal with being sick, but they also have to cope with some pretty tough treatments. Chemotherapy means sitting in a hospital room for hours, missing school, sports, dance or other hobbies. It can also make kids feel tired and crummy. Here are a few things that can help:

The body needs its strength during chemo, so be sure to eat nutritious foods. If you don't feel like eating, try breaking up meals into small high-protein, high-calorie snacks (like peanut butter, cheese, or yogurt) throughout the day.

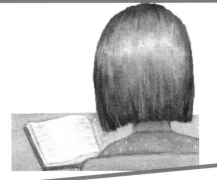

Tell close family members how you feel about cancer and chemotherapy. It's normal to feel angry, frustrated, sad, or scared.

Child Life Specialists are people who help children and their families deal with a serious medical illness. They can share tips for coping with the challenges that many young cancer patients experience.

Keeping up with homework is important during cancer treatment. It's a reminder that there is life beyond cancer. Doing homework can provide a sense of accomplishment and make it easier to start school again when the time is right.

Take favorite books, books on CD, movies, video games or magazines with you to chemotherapy. Doing an activity you enjoy will take your mind off the treatment and pass the time more quickly.

If you're feeling well enough, invite friends to visit with you. Spending time with friends can help life feel normal again.

Preventing Cancer When You Grow Up

No one knows how to prevent childhood cancer, but there are ways to try to protect against cancer when you grow up. While anyone can get cancer, people with a healthy lifestyle are less likely to get it as they get older. This lifestyle includes eating healthy foods, watching your weight, and getting plenty of exercise. Children who make healthy choices are more likely to have healthy habits when they grow up.

 Eat lots of brightly colored fruits and vegetables, especially those that are high in antioxidants: berries, broccoli, tomatoes, red grapes, spinach, carrots, oranges, cherries, beets, red bell peppers.

 Eat more whole-grains: whole-wheat bread instead of white; brown rice and pastas; oatmeal and other whole-grain cereals.

Eat less red meat, such as hamburgers and eat more chicken and fish.

 Exercise for about an hour on most days of the week: bike riding, playing games outside, walking, running, and sports of all kinds.

Find the Healthy Habits

Look for foods and activities that can be part of a healthy lifestyle. Select the healthy habit from each of the two choices. Then use the first letter of each healthy habit and unscramble the letters to find out what healthy habits make you.

Swimming or Watching TV	Eating a Cookie or a Tomato
Eating Oatmeal or a Donut for breakfast	Eating a Lollipop or a Nectarine
Eating Green beans or a Brownie	Riding a bike or Playing a video game

Answer: Strong

For Amy B.—SN

For Sunshine—KR

Thanks to Michael W. Smith, MD, Chief Medical Editor at WebMD, for verifying the information in this book.

A portion of the profits of this book are contributed to the ASCEND Foundation. In addition, the author is donating a portion of her royalties to the Make-a-Wish Foundation.

Champ's Story and an accompanying stuffed animal golden retriever are an educational and awareness initiative of the ASCEND Foundation, a non-profit organization, partnered with Sylvan Dell Publishing. It is ASCEND's vision to introduce the cancer book with cancer-related teaching activities for children into school systems. By utilizing the fun, fictional book, along with the stuffed version of its main character, Champ; teachers, parents, and caregivers will be able to educate children on social concerns and treatment protocols for cancer in a way to which young children can relate.

The ASCEND Foundation is a volunteer 501(c)(3) registered non-profit with a track record of initiatives designed to make a measureable difference in the battle against cancer. Its most recent initiative, "Gabe's Chemo Duck" provided a similar educational companion, free of charge to child oncology facilities across the country, as well as several oncology facilities in Europe. ASCEND will use all donations to fund "Champ the Cancer Companion" initiative with a vision to *Change the future of Cancer One Child at a Time.*"

If you or your organization would like to sponsor a "Cancer Companion" package for a child, a school, or for children's cancer centers in your area, please go to http://www.ascendfoundation.org or contact the office directly at 843-225-4055.

Publisher's Cataloging-In-Publication Data

North, Sherry.

Champ's story : dogs get cancer too! / by Sherry North ; illustrated by Kathleen Rietz.

p. : col. ill. ; cm.

Summary: A story of a young boy whose dog is diagnosed with cancer. The boy becomes a loving caretaker to his dog, who undergoes the same types of treatments as a human under similar circumstances. Includes "For Creative Minds" educational section.

ISBN: 978-1-60718-077-7 (hardcover)

ISBN: 978-1-60718-088-3 (paperback)

Also available as eBooks featuring auto-flip, auto-read, 3D-page-curling, and selectable English and Spanish text and audio

Interest level: 004-009

Grade level: P-4

ATOS™ Level: 2.9

Lexile Level: 510 Lexile Code: AD

1. Dogs--Juvenile fiction. 2. Cancer--Treatment--Juvenile fiction.
3. Cancer in animals--Juvenile fiction. 4. Human-animal relationships--
Juvenile fiction. 5. Dogs--Fiction. 6. Cancer--Treatment--Fiction.
I. Rietz, Kathleen. II. Title.

PZ10.3.N67 Ch 2010

[Fic]   2010921909

Manufactured in China, June, 2010
This product conforms to CPSIA 2008
First Printing

Sylvan Dell Publishing
976 Houston Northcutt Blvd., Suite 3
Mt. Pleasant, SC 29464

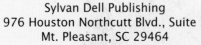